Classic

The Adventures of Tom Sawyer

Written by Cynthia Kennedy Henzel / Based on characters by Mark Twain

 CARAMEL TREE

CHAPTER 1

Tom Paints a Fence

Tom sat on an overturned wooden box with a long-handled brush in his hand, a large bucket of white paint next to him, and a sad feeling in his heart. He looked down the long length of unpainted board fence and sighed. All the other boys were playing ball or swimming. He was expected to spend this lovely sunny day painting a fence. It was a horrible way to spend a Saturday.

Tom lived with his Aunt Polly and his brother Sid. They had a small, neat house that overlooked the mighty Mississippi River. It was Aunt Polly who had assigned this hated chore, for

no good reason that Tom could see. He had torn his clothes

somewhat while fighting with the new boy, Jeff Thatcher. He

had come home late and tried to sneak in through a window.

But that was what boys did! All boys fought and got dirty.

Well, all boys but Sid. Tom suspected he only acted sweet to

make Tom look bad.

Tom dipped his brush into the bucket and slapped some

white paint on the fence. He groaned and sat back down. It was

so unfair! He hated working alone. Worse, the other boys would

soon come by and make fun of his misery.

That's when Tom had a brilliant idea. He grabbed his brush and began working intensely. Minutes later, the first of his friends came by.

"Guess you won't be swimming today," laughed Ben.

Tom kept working eagerly as if he hadn't noticed the other boy.

Ben came closer. "Got to work?" He laughed again and pulled a juicy apple from his pocket.

'I sure would like to have that apple,' thought Tom. But, he concentrated on his task all the harder.

"It's hot today," added Ben. "Glad I'm going swimming," he teased.

Tom turned around and pretended he was surprised to see Ben. "Oh! It's you Ben. I didn't notice you," he said.

"I'm going swimming," repeated Ben. "Don't you wish you could go, too?" He laughed and tossed the apple from hand to hand. "Or maybe you'd rather work?"

Tom dipped his brush into the bucket. "Why do you call this work?"

"Isn't *that* work?" Ben pointed at the fence.

Tom ran the brush down the fence. "Maybe it is and maybe it isn't."

"You mean you *like* it?" Ben looked curious.

Tom stepped back to admire his work. "How often does a boy get to paint a fence? Not often, I think."

Ben paused. It was true. He had never painted a fence. And Tom made it look like a fun thing to do. "Can I try it?" asked Ben.

"Oh, no!" said Tom. "I couldn't do that! Aunt Polly is very particular about this fence."

"Please," begged Ben. "I'd let you help if it was me."

"Well, I don't know..." Tom pretended to hesitate. He knew his plan was starting to work.

"Let me try and I'll give you my apple."

'Ah-ha!' thought Tom. He slowly gave Ben the brush. "It has to be done just right."

"I'll be really careful," promised Ben as he handed his apple to Tom.

Tom sat down on his wooden box and munched on the apple as Ben worked.

Soon, other boys came by. One by one, Tom allowed them to buy a chance to paint the fence. He sat back and watched. Before long, the job was done and Tom had three glass marbles, a bent key (to an unknown lock), and an Indian arrowhead.

As soon as the other boys left the yard, Tom ran to Aunt Polly. "Can I go out and play now?" he asked.

"Are you finished?" asked Aunt Polly, looking out the window.

"It's all done!" said Tom proudly.

"Now, Tom," cautioned Aunt Polly. "Lying is an awful sin."

"It's true!"

Aunt Polly knew Tom hated work. She went out to look for herself, thinking she'd be surprised to see the job half done. She was amazed to see the whole fence done with three coats of white paint!

"I'm sorry, Tom," she said. "I guess it's true that you can work when you want to." She went to the kitchen to find Tom an apple for a reward. As she searched, Tom grabbed a doughnut and stuffed it into his pocket while she wasn't looking.

As Aunt Polly sent him on his way, Tom spotted Sid in the yard. He picked up a ball of dried mud and pelted his brother. Then, Tom vanished over the back fence before Aunt Polly could catch him.

This was turning out to be a delightful Saturday after all.

CHAPTER 2

The Sugar Bowl

Tom had a fine afternoon playing soldiers with his friends. His best friend, Joe Harper, led one army. Tom led the other. These two great generals sat on a hill and commanded while the smaller boys fought. Soon, Tom's men won a great battle. The fighting was over for the day, so Tom headed home.

He decided to go by the home of Jeff Thatcher, the boy who had been responsible for getting him in trouble for fighting. Jeff was new in town. Tom was doing his duty to help the new boy understand who ran things. He suspected that Jeff might need another pounding.

Jeff Thatcher lived in the finest house in St. Petersburg, Missouri. His father was a judge. As Tom idled outside the fence, looking for his enemy, he saw a new girl in the garden. She had blue eyes and yellow hair in two long braids. She wore a white dress embroidered with flowers.

Tom fell instantly in love. His old girlfriend, Amy, fell from his heart. He watched until this new angel noticed him.

At once, Tom pretended he did not see her. He began to show off. He ran around, did somersaults, and hung from trees. When he glanced her way, however, she was walking away. Feeling rejected, he leaned against the fence.

The girl climbed the steps to the porch. She picked a flower and tossed it across the fence, and then went inside.

Tom pretended not to notice. He slowly eased closer until he could reach the flower. He picked it up with his bare toes, lifted his foot back, and swiftly took the scrunched up flower and put it into his pocket. He was in love!

At supper that night, Tom was scolded for throwing dried

mud at his brother. He didn't mind. His heart was filled with love. Instead of feeling ashamed about his deed, he tried to sneak some extra sugar from the sugar bowl. Aunt Polly smacked his knuckles.

"Hey!" cried Tom. "You don't beat Sid when he takes extra sugar."

"He isn't a constant headache," said Aunt Polly and gave him an extra smack.

As soon as Aunt Polly left for the kitchen, Sid reached over to sneak some extra sugar himself. However, he was busy smirking at Tom and his fingers knocked the bowl from the table. It broke with a crash!

Tom quietly leaned back. Sid was surely in big trouble now. Tom grinned as Aunt Polly returned. Her eyes narrowed and her teeth clenched. She lifted her hand as she approached the boys.

'Now, Sid is going to get it!' thought Tom.

Suddenly, Tom was sprawling on the floor. Aunt Polly lifted her hand to thump him again.

"Stop!" cried Tom. "Why are you hitting me? Sid did it!"

Aunt Polly paused with a confused look on her face.

Tom waited for an apology. *This is great!* His aunt's guilty conscience over hitting the wrong brother would be worth a lot of free mischief.

Aunt Polly did feel bad. But she knew Tom needed discipline and she didn't want to show weakness.

"You probably deserved a thumping for something," she said. "Get on out of here!"

Tom ran out. He knew in his heart that Aunt Polly did her best to bring him up properly. But he was furious at this injustice.

"This is proof that she doesn't care about me," he muttered to himself. "She'll be sorry if something happens to me." He pictured her crying at his funeral. It made him sad to think of such a thing. Then, he had a better idea. He would run off and become a pirate! That would make Aunt Polly sorry!

CHAPTER 3

Sitting Next to Girls

Tom stopped on the way to school on Monday morning to talk to his friend Huckleberry Finn. Tom wanted some company if he was going to be a pirate, and Huckleberry Finn was always ready for a new adventure.

"Hello, Huck Finn," called Tom.

"Hello, yourself!" answered Huck as he played with a poor overturned beetle. As usual, he was dirty and wore ragged clothes. Huck didn't have to go to school. His father, a drunkard and Huck's only family, didn't care what Huck did. All the parents in town would not allow their children to play

with him. This made Huck very popular with the boys.

"I'm running off to be a pirate, want to come?"

"What do pirates do?" asked Huck.

"They hunt for treasure and kidnap people," explained Tom. "It's grand adventure!"

"What do they do with the people after they kidnap them?" asked Huck.

"They demand money from their families to let them go."

"What if the family doesn't pay?" Huck flipped the beetle onto its feet and watched it scramble away.

"Then they make them walk on a plank. But, girls don't have to walk the plank. The girls are always beautiful and fall in love with the pirates," Tom said almost in a whisper.

"Sounds good," said Huck. "When are we leaving?"

"Soon," answered Tom. "We just need a few days to get our supplies," he added as he walked on, happy now that he had a partner.

Tom was dreaming of the adventures he would have as a pirate when he heard the school bell ring. He was late! Tom ran to school and hurried through the door.

"Thomas Sawyer!" said Mr. Dobbins. "Why are you late?"

Tom was about to tell a lie that would get him out of trouble. It had worked before. He could say that Aunt Polly was ill and he had to take care of her. That would get him out of trouble for being late. Then, he spotted long blonde hair on the girl's side of the room. All thoughts of pirates and lies left his head. The new girl with the blue eyes was here! There was an open seat beside her.

"I stopped to talk to Huck Finn, Sir." Tom made his voice bold and loud to be sure the new girl heard him.

The teacher turned red and picked up his cane. "That is a poor excuse!" he said. "Not only will you receive ten lashes, but you will then have to sit with the *girls*!"

The boys laughed. But Tom gladly took his lashes and went to sit by the new girl. Everything was going according to his plan.

The girl ignored him at first. Soon, he got her attention by drawing pictures on his slate.

"What's that?" whispered the girl.

"Nothing."

"Can I see?"

"No," said Tom, hiding the drawing with his arm. "It's no good."

The new girl leaned nearer. "Please?"

Finally, Tom showed her the house he had drawn. It was kind of crooked, but you could tell it was a house.

"Oh, that's beautiful," said the girl. "I wish I could draw."

"I can teach you," Tom offered.

The girl smiled, making Tom's heart beat faster. "What's your name?" he asked.

"Becky Thatcher," she replied. "I already know yours – Tom Sawyer!"

Tom sat straighter, proud that Becky knew who he was.

Tom drew more pictures for Becky. Before long, she agreed to meet him at lunch. They found a quiet place in the school room after all the other children went outside. Tom sat close by her side.

"Have you ever been engaged, Becky?"

"No," said Becky. "What is it?"

"It's when two people are going to get married," explained Tom.

"Oh! How do you get engaged?"

"Well, I whisper something in your ear. Then, you whisper it back," Tom said softly.

"I – I guess I could do that."

Tom leaned close and whispered in her ear. Becky turned pink.

"Now, you whisper it back," said Tom.

"Okay, but you have to promise not to tell. Close your eyes."

Tom obeyed and Becky leaned near. "I – love – you," she said.

"Now, are we engaged?"

"Almost," answered Tom. "We just have to kiss."

By and by, Becky agreed. Tom kissed her.

"Now, it's done!" said Tom. "And, you kiss even better than

Amy..."

Tom realized his mistake too late.

"You've been engaged before!" cried Becky.

"It was nothing," said Tom.

Becky wouldn't listen. She started crying.

Tom was miserable. "Aw, Becky..."

Becky cried harder.

"Please stop! I'll give you my favorite thing!" He took out a

glass marble from his pocket and handed it to her.

Becky threw it to the floor and cried harder.

Tom marched out of the school. Girls were so unreasonable!

Becky would be sorry for giving him up! Now, he was

determined to be a pirate.

CHAPTER 4

The Graveyard

Tom headed for the woods and soon ran into Huck again. This time Huck was swinging a dead black cat by its tail. Tom was curious.

"What are you doing with that cat?" asked Tom.

"I'm practicing my aim so I can hit the devil with it," explained Huck.

Tom was even more curious. "Hit the devil? Why do you want to do that?"

"Why? To get rid of a wart," explained Huck.

"How's that work?"

"Easy. You go to the graveyard at midnight after someone wicked was buried. When the devil comes to take him, you throw the cat after the devil and say, 'Devil follow corpse, cat follow devil, wart follow cat!' That's it."

"Sounds right. When are you going to do it?" asked Tom.

"Tonight. I figure the devil will be coming after old Hoss Williams tonight. You want to come?"

Tom couldn't resist this adventure. "Sure!" he replied.

Tom sneaked out of his house at midnight while Aunt Polly and Sid slept soundly. He had done it many times before so he knew exactly how to sneak out without making a sound.

It was a dark night, and very, very quiet. Tom met up with Huck as planned, and they crept into the dark graveyard. They tip-toed softly over the graves, each one marked by a wooden plaque. Both boys were thinking this was a bad idea. But, neither one of them was willing to admit it first.

As they got near the new grave of Hoss Williams, they saw

a light flickering. It was a lantern coming closer.

Tom pulled his friend behind a bush.

"There are three devils," Huck whispered. "This is awful! Can you start praying, Tom?"

Tom started praying, Huck shivering beside him.

"Shh! Wait a minute," whispered Huck. "They're humans! I hear Muff Potter's voice. He sounds drunk, as usual."

The men got nearer. A second voice joined the first. Tom's eyes opened wide. "That's Injun Joe!" Tom pointed. He knew Injun Joe was a criminal, suspected of murdering several men, and he did not want to run into him in daylight let alone in the dark.

"What are they doing?" whispered Huck.

The three men stopped at the grave just feet from where the boys hid. Now, the third man spoke up. "Here it is. Start digging."

"That's Doc Robinson!" said Tom.

"Hurry, the moon may come out soon," continued the young doctor. "We don't want anyone to see us!"

Tom and Huck watched Muff Potter and Injun Joe dig until their shovels hit the wooden coffin. They opened the lid. The moon appeared as they lifted out the corpse. They dumped it into a nearby wheelbarrow and covered it with a blanket. Muff Potter tied the corpse on with a rope and cut off the end of the rope with his knife.

"Okay, Doc," said Injun Joe. "If you want more help you owe another five dollars."

"Sounds right!" agreed Potter.

"What! I paid in advance!" exclaimed the doctor. "Now you want more?"

"That's right," growled Injun Joe. "I remember your father calling the Sheriff when I came to your door asking for something to eat. Now, you're going to pay!" He shook his fist in the young Doctor's face.

Dr. Robinson punched him in the jaw.

Potter dropped his knife to help Injun Joe. Dr. Robinson pulled the wooden plaque free from the ground and swung it at Potter, knocking him into the open grave.

Injun Joe grabbed the dropped knife. "This will teach you!" he cried. He leaped up and stabbed the doctor. The man fell over dead.

Injun Joe looked down at the unconscious Muff Potter. He put the bloody knife in Potter's hand. "It's your knife so everyone will believe you murdered the doctor," Injun Joe laughed. "And, you were so drunk you won't remember yourself."

Tom and Huck sneaked away before they could be spotted. They ran like the devil was after them. The truth is, Injun Joe was as close to a devil as Tom could imagine. Fortunately, the boys got away without being seen. They stopped at the edge of the woods to catch their breath.

"We've got to tell someone!" panted Tom.

"We can't do that!" exclaimed Huck. "If Injun Joe finds out we saw him murder the doctor, we're as good as dead ourselves."

"That's true," said Tom. "We've got to keep quiet. Injun Joe will stick a knife in us just like he did Doc Robinson."

Tom was troubled. He liked Muff Potter and hated to see him falsely accused. *'Surely, the Sheriff will see that Muff Potter is being set up,'* he thought. Meanwhile, they had to protect themselves.

"We should swear to each other to keep quiet," suggested Tom.

Huck agreed, so they pricked their thumbs and swore on blood to keep quiet.

"Might be a good time to start our pirate gang," said Tom.

Huck nodded. "Be good to be far away until they get Injun Joe locked up."

"I'll get Joe Harper to come with us, and we'll leave tomorrow night," said Tom. Joe Harper was Tom's best friend at school. Tom wouldn't want to go on a great adventure without him. It was only on the way home that he realized that tomorrow night was really *tonight*. The sun was about to rise.

By mid-morning the murder was discovered, and Muff Potter was arrested. The town was full of rumors, but the boys kept quiet. Tom felt bad, especially when he saw Injun Joe talking to the Sheriff.

'Was Injun Joe telling the Sheriff that he'd seen Muff Potter kill Dr. Robinson?' Tom wanted to set the record straight. But he had sworn to keep silent.

CHAPTER 5

Pirates

Tom met up with Huck and Joe Harper by the river at midnight. Joe had brought some ham he'd stolen from the kitchen. Tom had some bacon. Huck had a skillet and knife. They stole a raft, loaded their provisions, and set off down the river.

The three new pirates landed on an island just as the sun came up. They hid their raft and then set up camp. After a long morning nap, they built a fire and ate breakfast. Then, they set out to explore.

The island was large; half a mile wide and several miles long. The boys hiked and swam. They played at fighting invaders,

then swam some more. They hunted for treasure until they got tired, then napped. They woke up and fished. They ate fresh fish over an open fire for supper.

By sundown, they all agreed that the pirate life was the best life there was.

The second day was much the same. But by the third morning all the boys were thinking of home.

Joe was the first to say it out loud. "I miss my family," he said. "I think I want to go back."

Tom and Huck scoffed. "You're just a baby!"

BOOM! BOOM! Suddenly, the air was full of noise!

"It's too loud for guns," cried Joe. "I think it's cannons!"

The three hurried to the beach and hid behind large rocks.

BOOM!

Upriver they saw a boat. From the boat, cannons were being fired!

"I know what they're doing," exclaimed Tom. "Someone's drowned, and they're looking for them. The noise makes the body come to the top."

"I wonder who drowned?" asked Huck.

"We did!" exclaimed Joe. "Our folks think we drowned!"

The boys agreed this must be right. They felt bad now to have worried everyone in town, especially their families.

"We have to go back," said Joe.

Tom and Huck agreed this was the right thing to do.

"But let's wait another day," said Tom. "I have a great idea!"

The next night the boys set off in the raft. By morning, they had reached shore. They hiked to town. The church bells began to ring as they got close.

"Hurry!" said Tom. "We're going to be late."

They crept into the church and hid in the back. The preacher was giving their eulogy. "They were fine boys," he said, wiping away a tear. "They were young men filled with promise!"

Tom saw Aunt Polly and Sid in the church with tears running down their faces. "I loved him so!" sobbed Aunt Polly. Beside them, Joe's parents were crying just as hard. "How will I live without my Joe?" moaned Joe's mother. Everyone in the church was crying now.

Tom, Joe and Huck marched out of the shadows.

There were cries of joy and hugs as the townsfolk realized the boys were alive. Aunt Polly practically smothered Tom with hugs.

Huck turned away. He had no family.

CHAPTER **6**

Crime and Punishment

Times were grand! Tom, Huck and Joe were heroes among the other boys. Tom told the tale of their days as pirates over and over. With each telling, the boys faced greater danger and hardship. Plus, Aunt Polly felt guilty about her part in making Tom run away and was as sweet as honey.

Still, Tom arrived back at school in a dreary mood. Becky was still mad at him even though she had said she was glad he wasn't dead.

It was early, but Tom decided to go inside the classroom and sit awhile. He opened the door. His heart fluttered. Becky stood alone at the teacher's desk with an open book. Her back was turned so she didn't notice Tom.

Tom immediately guessed what she was doing. Whenever the students were busy, Mr. Dobbins unlocked his desk drawer and pulled out a special book to read. Every student was curious about that book, but Mr. Dobbins always kept the drawer locked.

Tom tiptoed across the room and looked over Becky's shoulder. She was looking at the title page: Professor Somebody's Anatomy. Becky turned the page and revealed a color picture of a human figure – and it was naked!

At that moment, Tom's shadow fell across the page. Becky gasped. In her hurry to close the book, she accidentally tore the picture.

Immediately, Becky started crying. "I know you're going to tell on me," she sobbed. "I'm going to be whipped – and I've never been whipped in school before!" she cried harder.

Tom was puzzled. He got whipped regularly and thought

nothing of it. "I'm not going to tattle, Becky," he said. Then, he went outdoors to join the boys.

It was difficult for Tom to study that morning. He kept stealing glances at Becky. The girl looked miserable.

Finally, Mr. Dobbins settled the class, pulled out the book and opened the cover. Then he jumped up and glared at the students. "Who tore this book?" he demanded.

The room was silent. No one moved.

"Joe Harper," barked Mr. Dobbins, "did you tear this book?"

"No, sir!" said Joe.

"Becky Thatcher! Did you tear this book?" Becky's face was white with terror. Her whole body quaked.

Tom couldn't stand it. "I did it!" he shouted.

Everyone stared at him in amazement. Why would he admit to such a thing?

Tom walked to the front of the room to take his punishment. As he passed Becky, he saw the surprise and thankfulness in her eyes. Inspired by his own greatness, he took the whipping without a sound.

For many weeks, time went along smoothly. Then, the peace was disturbed by the beginning of Muff Potter's trial. It didn't look good for the accused man.

Tom felt terrible. He knew that Muff Potter was innocent but couldn't tell anyone without breaking his word. So, he went in search of Huck. "Have you told anybody about – about what happened?" asked Tom.

"Of course not!" said Huck.

"We've got to do something," said Tom. "Injun Joe told the Sheriff he saw Muff do the killing. They'll find Muff guilty and hang him for sure."

Huck's eyes got wide. "You swore you wouldn't say anything! You've got a place to stay, but Injun Joe will hunt me down!" Huck drew an imaginary knife across his throat.

"We can't let an innocent man hang!"

Huck hung his head. "It's a bad, awful thing. He's always been good to me. But, nothing we can do."

The boys talked awhile longer, but they could fi gure no way out.

Tom, his heart heavy, went to visit Muff Potter in jail. It was a tiny building on the edge of town. As he got near, he saw Muff looking out the little window of his cell.

"I'm sure glad to see you, Tom!" cried the prisoner. "It's mighty lonesome out here." The man looked so grateful to have a visitor that Tom could hardly stand it.

Tom handed an apple through the bars. "Hate to see you locked up," said Tom.

"Guess I deserve it," sighed Muff. "I don't remember it, but they say I killed young Doc Robinson."

"I don't believe you'd hurt anybody!" declared Tom.

Muff shook his head sadly. "I'd never hurt anyone on purpose. The fact is that I was drinking and Doc Robinson is dead. It doesn't matter if I remember killing him or not."

Tom could hardly stand to keep quiet. But, he'd sworn to Huck he wouldn't tell about seeing Injun Joe. He could only hope that the Sheriff would somehow figure out the truth.

The trial started the next morning, and each day it looked worse for Muff Potter. The Sheriff told about finding Muff's bloody knife. Then, he told about finding Muff himself passed out nearby. Several people took the stand to say what a fine young man Dr. Robinson had been.

When they were all done, Judge Thatcher asked Muff's lawyer if he had questions. The lawyer said, "No."

Next, Injun Joe swore on the Bible that he'd seen Muff stab the doctor. "I saw it with my own eyes." He tried to convince the Judge.

Sitting in the courtroom, Tom and Huck waited for God to strike him down. Surely, the Lord wouldn't let Injun Joe get away with lying after swearing on the Bible.

But nothing happened. The judge asked Muff's lawyer if he had questions for the witness.

"Not at this time," said the lawyer.

The judge looked surprised. "Are you sure you have no questions?"

"I have no questions," said the lawyer.

"We will break until tomorrow," said Judge Thatcher.

The next morning the courtroom was packed with people. It looked like Muff Potter was a goner.

"Are there any witnesses for the defense?" asked Judge Thatcher.

"We have only one witness. We call - Tom Sawyer."

All eyes were on Tom as he walked up and swore to tell the truth.

"Now, Tom," began the lawyer. "Where were you on the night of Dr. Robinson's murder?"

Tom glanced at Injun Joe. His voice failed.

"Tom?" said Judge Thatcher. "Answer the question."

Tom took a deep breath. "In the graveyard!"

A contemptuous smile crossed the face of Injun Joe.

"Were you near the grave of Hoss Williams?"

"Yes, sir. I was as close as I am to you."

"Were you hidden?"

"Yes, we were behind the trees with a dead cat."

The watchers in the courtroom laughed, but Judge Thatcher motioned them to silence.

"We will produce the cat's skeleton as evidence," the lawyer told the judge. He turned back to Tom. "Someone was with you?"

"Yes."

"Never mind who it was," said the lawyer. "What did you see?"

Tom told the whole story, but left out Huck's name. His words became rushed as he got near the end. "Muff Potter fell," he explained, "then Injun Joe jumped up with the knife..."

Crash!

Injun Joe sprang out the window and was gone!

CHAPTER 7

The Haunted House

Tom stayed close to home for the next week. He was a hero again. Even Huck said he was brave and was grateful that Tom hadn't given out his name. Tom basked in the praise, but found himself looking into every shadow for his enemy. However, it seemed that Injun Joe was gone.

As the days went by with no sign of the escaped murderer, Tom began to feel his confinement. Soon, he was looking for Huck in search of new adventure.

Tom found his friend fishing near the dock. They sat and threw stones into the river. Tom missed their pirate days.

"I think we should go look for treasure," suggested Tom.

Huck looked interested. "What kind of treasure?"

"Pirate treasure! Like gold and diamonds and such."

"Don't know what I'd do with diamonds," said Huck, "but I wouldn't mind having some gold. You know where to find some?"

"We've got to dig it up," explained Tom. "Pirates bury their treasure."

"Where do they bury it?"

"It's always under some strange shaped tree or maybe in a haunted house." He snapped his fingers. "I know just the place. Everybody says that old place in the woods out past Widow Douglas's house is haunted."

Huck looked worried. "I don't like haunted houses. Besides, every time I go by the Widow Douglas's place, she stares like there's something wrong with me."

"You want the gold or not?"

Huck sighed. "Let's go now before it gets dark."

Most of the old houses in town had been torn down or fixed up. But, the deserted house outside of town was known to be haunted so nobody messed with it. Tom and Huck had no problem finding a way in through a broken window.

Huck tiptoed past the stairs to the fireplace, peering into shadowy corners. "Where do you think it is?" he whispered.

"They wouldn't just leave it lying around," scoffed Tom. "Pirates always bury their treasure in a trunk. My guess is it's under a loose floorboard."

The boys tapped along the floor looking for a board that sounded loose.

Suddenly, Huck stopped. "Listen, Tom! What's that?"

Tom heard it, too.

Voices.

"It's ghosts!" whispered Huck frantically. "We've got to get out of here."

Tom put a hand on Huck to keep him from dashing out the door. "Quiet! It's coming from outside, and one of those ghosts sounds a lot like Injun Joe!"

"This must be his hideout! We're goners, Tom!"

"Hide!" hissed Tom.

They looked around the room. There was nowhere to hide. "Upstairs!" cried Tom. He led the way. They crept up the old staircase, avoiding the creaking, rotting boards the best they could. They made it to the top as the door opened below.

Tom looked through a knothole in the floor. Two men stepped in. One of them was Injun Joe. The other had to be his new partner.

Both boys shivered with fright. They were trapped. If the men came upstairs, there was nowhere to hide and no way to escape. Tom pressed his ear to the floor to listen.

"So? Where's it at?" asked the stranger.

Tom heard footsteps cross the floor to the fireplace, then a scraping noise. "Behind this loose stone," said Injun Joe. "Help me move it."

The men groaned as if moving something heavy.

"Here it is," said Injun Joe. "Help me lift it out."

There was more groaning. Tom pressed his eye to the hole. They were lifting a trunk from a hole behind the fireplace.

Indignantly, Tom turned to whisper in Huck's ear. "They found our treasure!" Then, losing his balance, he thumped a knee down on the floor. The boys froze and looked at each other in panic.

"What was that?" said Injun Joe.

"Somebody's up there!" said his partner.

"Well, there'll be another ghost haunting this place in a short while," said Injun Joe. He bounded up the stairs.

Crash! The old stairway was too rotten for a full grown man. It splintered and fell, taking Injun Joe with it.

Injun Joe picked himself up and glared at the ruined staircase. "Don't matter," he grumbled. "Just grab a side of this trunk and let's get out of here."

Tom and Huck waited until they couldn't hear the men's voices. Then, they waited longer to make sure they didn't come back. Finally, they climbed down holding onto bits of the broken stairway.

Tom felt braver now that they were gone. "That was our treasure," he complained. "Injun Joe just stole it."

"He sure did," agreed Huck. "But we aren't going to see it again. That's for sure."

The boys peered cautiously out before they left the house.

Tom hoped the outlaw had only come back to get the treasure and was gone for good since it wasn't likely that he'd forgotten who'd testified against him. But no one spotted Injun Joe again in the coming week, and Tom began to relax.

CHAPTER **8**

Lost in the Cave

The next week, Tom's class went on a class picnic. They traveled on a boat down the river and spent the day playing and eating. In the afternoon, the class set out to explore a nearby cave.

Tom was familiar with the cave. He and his friends had explored the parts of it near the entrance. No one knew anything about the deeper areas. The dark chambers and corridors went on for miles. It was rumored that people who had tried to go too far inside were never seen again.

Inside the cave, Mr. Dobbins warned the children to stay close.

At first the children obeyed. But the huge cave was too alluring. A few brave boys and girls went deeper, holding candles to light the way and being careful not to go too far.

Becky seemed uncomfortable in the dark so Tom held his candle in front of her. He was really glad they were friends again and had told no one about taking her punishment for tearing the book.

After a time, Tom took Becky's hand and led her down a long, twisting tunnel.

"We'll get lost!" squealed Becky.

"Don't worry," bragged Tom. "I know all about these caves."

They came to a huge cavern with hundreds of stalactites hanging from the ceiling.

"It's beautiful!" cried Becky. Her voice echoed from wall to wall.

Tom held the candle high. The cavern was so large they couldn't see the other side.

They climbed from rock to rock deeper into the cavern.

Occasionally, Tom saw a tunnel leading off the huge cavern. One of the tunnels went behind a flow of rock that glittered with moisture.

"Let's go down here," Tom suggested.

"Don't you think we should go back?" asked Becky.

Tom looked at his candle. Half of it was gone. "I guess we should," he agreed. He looked across the huge cavern, trying to decide exactly which tunnel they had come from.

"You know how to get back, don't you, Tom?" Becky said with a tremor in her voice.

"Sure!" said Tom. "It's that one, right over there." But he didn't sound too certain.

Tom led the way and they walked quickly back. They noticed new tunnels that they hadn't noticed before. But, they tried to stay in the main tunnel. After what seemed like a very long time, Tom slowed. He could feel Becky's hand quivering in his.

He took her candle and blew it out. Shadows swarmed closer.

Suddenly, the cave felt much darker and colder.

"Why did you do that?" cried Becky. The tremor in Becky's voice told Tom that she suspected the truth.

"Sorry, Becky. We need to save a candle. We're lost."

Tom and Becky wandered through tunnel after tunnel. Nothing looked familiar. The last of their candles burned down. They walked in darkness, praying that they did not fall off a cliff or into a deep hole. Hours or days later – it was impossible to tell – they came to a small pool of fresh water. Becky sat down, and Tom brought her water in his hands. She drank, but refused to get up.

"I can't go on," sighed Becky. "I'm too hungry and tired." She curled into a ball. "It's so cold in here, Tom."

"Don't worry, Becky," Tom assured her. "I'll find a way out. The others have to be looking for us by now."

Tom left Becky and felt his way around the walls of the cave. He found a tunnel and walked slowly, praying he would find a way out. To his delight, he saw a faraway glow. *'That must be the rescue team,'* he thought as he hurried toward the glow.

Fortunately, he stopped just before he fell into a hole. It was too dark to tell how deep it was. Tom leaned forward until he could see around the corner. A man held a candle. Tom sucked in his breath. It was Injun Joe! He was hiding the treasure chest behind a rock!

Tom backed away cautiously. Silently, he went back to where Becky waited.

He found the girl asleep. "Becky, get up!" Tom whispered urgently. But the girl was too weak and did not respond. Tom took her arm and wrapped it around his shoulder. He had to move her immediately. Injun Joe might come this way and find them. Tom was exhausted, too, but he stood and carried the unconscious Becky down another tunnel.

As he felt his way down the tunnel, he noticed that the shadows were less dark along one side. He crept ahead.

It got lighter.

He went faster.

Then, sunlight! Tom had found a way out.

Tom carried the unconscious Becky out of the cave and down toward the river. They found some fishermen. When the men realized they were the children who'd been lost for two days, they gladly took them home.

CHAPTER **9**

Riches

Tom was a hero once again although it was several weeks before Becky was well enough for company.

"I wanted to be the first to thank you, Tom," said Judge Thatcher. "Your courage saved my daughter."

Tom scuffed a shoe on the porch to hide his embarrassment. After all, he was the one who had gotten them lost in the beginning.

"The good thing is," continued the Judge, "we won't ever have children lost in there again. I've had an iron door installed at the entrance with three locks." He held up the keys. "No one's going in that cave again!"

"But Injun Joe's in there!" Tom cried out. "You've trapped him inside!"

Judge Thatcher sent word to the Sheriff. Soon, half the town was headed to the cave. A half hour later, they climbed the path to the cave entrance.

"Stand back!" shouted the Sheriff.

Judge Thatcher unlocked the locks. Several men came forward and pulled open the heavy door.

The crowd gasped.

Injun Joe lay curled inside. He had died from thirst and starvation.

Tom had told no one about the secret cave entrance. Now, he was eager to see Huck. He found his friend at the Widow Douglas's house. Huck had been very sick. He was better now but was lucky the kind woman had cared for him. He was amazed when Tom told him about seeing Injun Joe in the cave.

Tom led Huck to the secret cave entrance from where he had escaped. They clambered down the tunnel to the room with the pool. Then, Tom led the way down the second tunnel to the chasm.

"This is it," said Tom. "The treasure's right across there."

"Maybe Injun Joe moved it," said Huck.

"It's too heavy for one man to move easily. Injun Joe could hardly push it behind the rocks by himself. I suspect his partner helped him bring it here, and then Injun Joe killed him so he'd have it all to himself."

They'd brought along some ropes. Now, they threw them across the chasm and slipped into Injun Joe's lair.

Huck looked around nervously. "You think Injun Joe's ghost may be haunting this place?"

Tom felt troubled at the thought. Then, he brightened and pointed at a cross marked in soot on the wall. "No ghost's going to haunt a place near a cross."

They both knew this was true. So, they went on and quickly

found the treasure chest. Huck held the candle high as Tom opened the lid.

Tom gasped and Huck almost dropped the candle. The chest was filled with coins. This was more money than anyone in town, even the banker, had ever seen. With much effort, Tom and Huck packed the coins in bags and carried them from the cave.

They took the fortune to Tom's house to count. Aunt Polly took charge of Tom's part of the money. She put it in the bank at a good interest to save for Tom's education. She allowed him a dollar a week for spending money. Tom was the richest boy in town!

The Widow Douglas became Huck's guardian. She gave Huck a fine home and taught him proper manners. Huck didn't like all the baths and having to go to school. But, he decided it was worth the trouble to have someone who loved him.